The
SECOND COMING OF
JESUS CHRIST 2022

The Second Coming of Jesus Christ 2022
Copyright © 2022 by Eddie Naylor Sr.

Published in the United States of America
ISBN   Paperback: 978-1-959761-26-6
ISBN   eBook: 978-1-959761-27-3

All rights reserved. No part of this publication may be reproduced, stored in a retrieval system or transmitted in any way by any means, electronic, mechanical, photocopy, recording or otherwise without the prior permission of the author except as provided by USA copyright law.

The opinions expressed by the author are not necessarily those of ReadersMagnet, LLC.

ReadersMagnet, LLC
10620 Treena Street, Suite 230 | San Diego, California, 92131 USA
1.619. 354. 2643 | www.readersmagnet.com

Book design copyright © 2022 by ReadersMagnet, LLC. All rights reserved.

Cover design by Ericka Obando
Interior design by Dorothy Lee

The
SECOND COMING OF
JESUS CHRIST 2022

"This Generation 2022 will be the time that will usher in the second coming of Jesus Christ!!!"

EDDIE LEE NAYLOR SR.

ReadersMagnet, LLC

THIS GENERATION 2022 WILL BE THE TIME THAT WILL USHER IN THE SECOND COMING OF JESUS CHRIST!!!!!!!!!!!!!!

The return of Jesus and the end time prophecies have been around ever since Christ went back to heaven, but they all turn into bitter disappointment. In fact, no one knows the exact date of the return of Jesus Christ. In this list, top latest End Times Predictions and return of Jesus and that miserably failed, includes numerous modern false prophets, religious believers or leaders, scientist…

Great Disappointment (William Miller, Millerites 1843-1844)

Although it was not officially endorsed by their leadership, many Millerites expected the Second Coming of Jesus to occur on April 28 or at the end of 1843.

When the prediction failed, William miller predicted another date, Mar 21, 1844, that Jesus would return. The disappointment of the second prediction was worse than the first one.

Mother Shipton (1881)

Ursula Southeil, better known as Mother Shipton, is said to have been an English soothsayer and prophetess. Her publications contained a number of prophecies: regional predictions and the End of the World.

400 years earlier, Mother Shipton claimed that the world would end in 1881: "The world to an end shall come. In eighteen hundred and eighty-one".

Jonas Wendell – 1873

In 1870, Wendell published his views in the booklet entitled The Present Truth, or Meat in Due Season, concluding that the Second Advent was sure to occur in 1873.

In case you don't remember, we are in 2015 now; Jesus is still yet to come.

Catholic Apostolic Church – 1901

This church, founded in 1831, claimed that Jesus would return by the time the last of its 12 founding members died. The last member died in 1901, and Jesus has not come.

The disappointment has led to a gradual decline in church membership. The organization is barley known in some parts of the worlds.

Ed Dobson, Timothy Dwight IV, Edgar Cayce, Isaac Newton, 2000

In his book The End: Why Jesus Could Return by A.D. 2000, Pastor Ed Dobson predicted the end would occur in 2000 with the second coming of Jesus.

Timothy Dwight IV, the President of Yale University, foresaw the beginning of Christ's Millennium by the year 2000.

The American mystic (psychic), Edgar Cayce, predicted Jesus Christ would return in the year 2000 as well.

If Newton was a true physicist and mathematician, surely he was a false prophet. In his book, Observations upon the Prophecies of Daniel, and the Apocalypse of St. John, he predicted Christ's Millennium would begin in the year 2000.

James Harmston, the leader of the True and Living Church of Jesus Christ of Saints of the Last Days, also had his prediction for Jesus to come in 2000, precisely in April 6, 2001.

Harold Camping – May 21, 2011; Oct 21, 2011

In 2001, Harold Camping claimed that the Rapture and Judgment Day would occur on May 21, 2011, and predicted the end of the world would arrive in five months later, on October 21, 2011.

I don't know where you are, but this is 2015 and Human beings are not in Heaven yet. Sadly, some people still believe his words, following him as a real man of God.

Ronald Weinland – Sep 29, 2011; May 27, 2012; May 18, 2013

Ronald Weinland is a former Worldwide Church of God (WCG) minister and founder of Church of God, Preparing for the Kingdom of God (COG-PKG).

He predicted the second coming of Christ on September 29, 2011. When his prediction failed to occur, he changed the date to May 27, 2012. Again, that prediction failed. He then moved the date to May 18, 2013. Being now out of false predictions, as excuse, he claims "a day with God is as a year".

As of today, Weinland is not in heaven or hell, he is in federal prison, after he was convicted of tax evasion in 2012 and sentenced to 3 1/2 years.

MORE DETAILING IN HIS FALSE PHOPHECY

Grigori Rasputin – Aug 23, 2013

Unlike the others, "prophet" Rasputin was more detailing in his false prophecy; maybe to get more attention.

He predicted a storm would hit the earth, causing a fire to destroy most life on land and Jesus Christ would return to earth to comfort those in distress.

No one knows the day or the hour of my return. In Mark 13:32, Jesus had been teaching his disciples about his return and says, "But concerning that day or that hour, no one knows, not even the angels in heaven, nor the Son, but only the Father."

ANOTHER FALSE TEACHER WAS DUPED

Another false teacher recently joined the historic cohort who've arrogantly thought they had figured out when Christ will return. This is tragic on two levels. First, there are many who were duped. Tons of people believed the prediction and invested time, energy, and money spreading it. Secondly, it's tragic that many will now move toward the opposite extreme. They suspected Jesus wouldn't return anytime soon and now see this false prediction as confirmation he really isn't. This is an equally tragic mistake. Jesus said a lot about his return and one of the overarching messages was His followers should keep themselves ready and waiting.

Here are 10 things Jesus really said about his return.

1. No one knows the day or the hour of my return.

In Mark 13:32, Jesus had been teaching his disciples about his return and says, "But concerning that day or that hour, no one knows, not even the angels in heaven, nor the Son, but only the Father." Luke records it this way, "You also must be ready, for the Son of Man is coming at an hour you do not expect." (Lk 12:40).

Jesus told his disciples even He didn't know exactly when He would return. At this point in history, God the Father knew the exact number of years, months, days and seconds until Christ would return and Jesus didn't. We need not speculate about future details Christ himself didn't know.

Also, Jesus applied this truth to their lives, "Be ready." Jesus didn't know if he would return in their lifetimes, but his command to them is his command to us almost 2,000 years later. Keep watch. Stay awake.

2. There will be several signs, increasing in intensity, as my return draws near.

Christ's followers should pay attention to the signs of his return. They should speculate about the exact day or hour but should pay attention to natural events and recognize the potential fulfillment of Christ's words as they happen.

Jesus promised there would be wars and rumors of wars, famines, earthquakes in various places (Matt 24:6-7). And also, "signs in sun and moon and stars, and on the earth distress of nations in perplexity because of the roaring of the sea and the waves, people fainting with fear and with foreboding of what is coming on the world. For the powers of the heavens will be shaken. And then they will see the Son of Man coming in a cloud with power and great glory" (Lk 21:25-27).

Additionally, Jesus used the term "birth pains" to describe these signs. Like the pain of childbirth, these signs will get more intense and frequent as the day draws close. When we see increasing numbers of earthquakes, tsunamis, tornadoes, and other natural disasters, Jesus instructs, "straighten up and raise your heads, because your redemption is drawing near" (Lk 21:28). Once again, Jesus instructs us to pay attention to the signs of His return in order to be ready when He comes.

3. Pray for the strength to escape the things that are going to take place.

In Luke 21:36, Jesus taught his followers, "But stay awake at all times, praying that you may have strength to escape all these things that are going to take place, and to stand before the Son of Man." From the context, the "escaping" Jesus refers to is escaping from the judgment and wrath God will bring upon those who have rejected Christ. Jesus teaches his disciples to pray for the strength to escape. Too many believe Christians will escape by default, but Jesus told his disciples to pray for strength to escape, and so we must.

4. It will seem like a normal day.

In Luke 17:26-30, Jesus compared the day the Son of Man will be revealed to God's judgment in the days of both Noah and Lot. In both these times, people were going about the normal business of life: eating, drinking, marrying, buying, selling, planting, and building. In the midst of this apparent normalcy, God's judgment and wrath fell. Jesus said this is what it will be like when He comes. It will be a great cosmic interruption that will be like lightning which "lights up the sky from one side to the other" (Lk 17:24).

5. I will repay everyone for what he has done.

In the last chapter of Revelation, Jesus told his followers He is coming and "bringing his recompense…to repay everyone for what he has done" (22:12). Matthew 25 describes the scene when Jesus will sit on his glorious throne and all nations will be gathered before him to be judged (31-33). All people will stand before Jesus and give account for what they did in life. How glorious it will be to stand confidently in the imputed righteousness of Christ in that day.

6. Not everyone who expects to make it into Christ's kingdom will.

Some of the most sobering words of Jesus are about those who will not be allowed to enter the kingdom of heaven. In Matthew 7:21-23, Jesus said, "Not everyone who says to me, 'Lord, Lord,' will enter the kingdom of heaven, but the one who does the will of my Father who is in heaven. On that day many will say to me, 'Lord, Lord, did we not prophesy in your name, and cast out demons in your name, and do many mighty works in your name?' And then will I declare to them, 'I never knew you; depart from me, you workers of lawlessness.'" What could be worse than hearing these words from Jesus?

At the end, there will be many people who will think they are in because of their ministry credentials. And Jesus will say, "I never knew you" and call them "workers of lawlessness." Their repentance was in word only. They acted like followers but didn't have a saving relationship with Christ based on faith and repentance as the foundation of their lives. Jesus said there will be many people in this terrifying condition, living their lives thinking they were in and finding out in the final analysis they weren't.

7. There will be great persecution and many will fall away.

Jesus promised great persecution would break out against his followers and would cause many to fall away (Matt 24:9-10). It's relatively easy to follow Christ when things are going well, but when times get tough we find out what we're made of. Is our faith in Christ only as strong as the comfort we enjoy? If God's enemies come and take everything will we cling to Christ or fall away? Jesus promised many would make the incomprehensible choice to fall away.

8. Because of lawlessness, the love of many will grow cold.

Jesus promised that sin would lure many away from Him (Matt 24:12). These are people who once loved Christ warmly who have cooled in their affections for Him. They've traded in their desires for Christ for worthless idols. Sex, money, power and other false gods have replaced the love of Christ in their hearts. Their love grows cold as they lose the war against temptations to sin. Stoking the heart's fiery love for Christ must include destroying the wet buckets of sin that can so quickly quench it. True Christ followers must repent often and much.

9. Be on your guard. Keep awake.

Jesus continually told his followers to stay awake, to watch their lives, and to be ready for his return. In Matthew, Jesus gave four parables to explain how and why his followers should be prepared for his coming: the homeowner and the thief (24:42-44); the good and wicked servants (24:45-51); the 10 virgins (25:1-13); and the talents (25:14-30). In each of these parables, Christ described readiness with working to complete the work Christ gave us, namely fulfilling the Great Commission. Every Christian is to diligently use the gifts and opportunities God provides to reach the world for Christ.

To be awake is to be ready and willing to do Christ's will. In Gethsemane, Jesus' disciples slept instead of joining Him in prayer. They weren't doing what Christ asked but slept. In the same way, many Christians today are asleep to Christ's will. They don't seek him or ask for his direction. Instead, like the disciples in the garden, they sleep. Hear the words of the prophet Isaiah, "Awake, awake, put on strength" (51:9).

Peter says it well, "The end of all things is at hand; therefore, be self-controlled and sober-minded for the sake of your prayers. Above all, keep loving one another earnestly, since love covers a multitude of sins" (1 Peter 4:7-8).

10. I am coming soon!

Four times in the book of Revelation, Jesus said to the churches, "I am coming soon!" (Rev 16:15; 22:7,12,20). It was originally meant as an encouraging word to 1st century Christians suffering by the hands of Rome and has continued to encourage Christ's followers throughout the ages. Christians in every generation are to hold tightly to the promise that Christ will return soon.

As the writer of Hebrews reminds, "Christ, having been offered once to bear the sins of many, will appear a second time, not to deal with sin but to save those who are eagerly waiting for him" (Heb

9:28). Like young children eagerly longing for Christmas morning, Christians eagerly wait for Christ to return. In doing so, we live out Paul's wonderful promise to the church in Thessalonica, "Then we who are alive, who are left, will be caught up together with them in the clouds to meet the Lord in the air, and so we will always be with the Lord" (1 Thess 4:17). Nothing is greater than to be with Jesus Christ always and forever.

THE SHAKING OF THE EARTH

When I was a little boy there was five of us sleeping in a regular bed. Dad had to go to work each morning in the winter time and it was very cold. Well each one of the boys had a morning to get up and make a fire. Well one morning dad called for one of us to make a fire so that mom could get up to cook breakfast so that he could go to work and we could go to school. He called and called but no one would would get up to make the fire. We all was hanging on and pulling the cover trying to keep warm. Finally, dad got tired of calling. He then got his big big belt and came in and start beating all of us. We all jumped up and started to make the fire. We refused him at first who was speaking until he got all of our attention with the belt he really shook us up!!!

See that you do not refuse him who is speaking. For if they did not escape when they refused him who warned them on earth, much less shall we escape if we reject him who warns from heaven. His voice then shook the earth; but now he has promised, "Yet once more I will shake not only the earth but also the heaven." This phrase, "Yet once more," <u>indicates the removal of what is shaken, as of what has been made, in order that what cannot be shaken may remain</u>. Therefore, let us be grateful for receiving a kingdom that cannot be shaken, and thus let us offer to God acceptable worship, with reverence and awe; for our God is a consuming fire. (Hebrews12:25-29)

This passage tends to sober us, because it speaks of the shaking of the heavens and of the earth. There is something chilling about the thought of the shaking of the earth.

A man told me a story he said a week or so ago, I was sitting with a certain person on the porch of his cabin on the shore of Lake Michigan.

As we were talking together, looking out over the waters of the lake, he said, "Do you see how close the shoreline is to the cabin? When we moved here ten years ago, the waters were forty to sixty feet further out. I asked, "What made the change?" He told me, "No one seems to know. When they built the St. Lawrence Seaway and opened the Great Lakes to ocean-going vessels, many thought that a great deal more water would go out to the ocean than before, and that the water level of the lakes would drop. The interesting thing is, the exact opposite has happened. Gradually the level of the Great Lakes has risen. [That represents a tremendous volume of water, for as many of you know, Lake Michigan is almost 500 miles long and some 60 to 100 miles wide. And it is only one of five Great Lakes.] But no one really seems to know what is causing it. The only explanation they can think of is that something must be causing the beds of the lakes slowly to rise or tilt." As I sat there I got an eerie feeling, and I looked around to see whether there was access up the hill behind us, if suddenly the process should accelerate!

PHYSICALLY SHAKING OF THE EARTH

The Scriptures speak of a time, as we draw near to the end, when there will be a physical shaking of the earth. In the book of Revelation, a key event, described repeatedly throughout that book of images and visions, is a great earthquake, so tremendous that the very foundations of the earth are shaken and every mountain and hill is removed from its place. That is a guide to the understanding of the book, for as you read through those visions, you find them returning again and again to the great earthquake which will wind up the course of human events in this age.

GOD SHOOK THE EARTH WHEN HE SPOKE

But when the writer of this passage speaks of God's shaking of the heavens and the earth, it is a different kind of shaking to which he is referring. He reminds the readers that once God shook the earth when he spoke from Mount Sinai in the giving of the Law. This was the time when the Law, coming to man, shook the nations of the world, shook their very foundations.

NOW THE WRITER IS QUOTING FROM THE PROPHET HAGGAI

Now, it is true that when God spoke from the mountain, the mountain itself shook and trembled like a leaf in the autumn wind, billowing smoke and fire. And the people were amazed and trembled with great fear when they saw this entire mountain shaking, as a symbol of the effect of the Law coming to men and nations throughout history.

And now the writer is quoting from the prophet Haggai, reminding them that there would come another shaking. "Yet once more," God says, "I will shake not only the earth but also the heaven." If you look back to the prophecy from which that was taken, <u>you will find that Haggai was looking forward to the coming of Messiah, the coming of Christ</u>. This will be the time, he says, when God will shake not only the earth but the heavens as well. And this will be a shaking which no one can avoid. The warning of this passage is, "Do not refuse him who is speaking, for there is no way to avoid the shaking that is to come."

PAUL FROM MAMERTIME DUNGEON IN ROME TO HIS YOUNG SON IN THE FAITH TIMOTHY

The last word we have from the hand of Paul, as he writes from the Maritime dungeon in Rome, to his young son in the faith, Timothy, is that most of his friends have forsaken him, that many to whom he ministered have turned away from him, and he sees all that he built apparently beginning to collapse. But he reminds Timothy that the Spirit of God had said expressly that in the latter days' perilous times should come. And he goes on to describe them—times of shaking, times when everything will be upset and all that men have counted as permanent and lasting will be overthrown, times of confusion and upheaval.

Eddie Naylor Sr.

LATTER DAYS JUST BEFORE RETURN OF CHRIST

Many people have taken the phrase "the latter days" to refer to the time just before the return of Christ. <u>But if you look at that phrase in other places in Scripture, especially in the book of Hebrews you find that "the latter days" or "the last days" refers to the entire age between the first and the second comings of Jesus.</u> We have been living in "the last days" since our Lord was here on earth. What the Spirit was saying is that, during this whole age, there would come repeated cycles of perilous times when God would shake the earth and the heavens, and things would be upset and confused, times of upheaval. <u>One of the comforting things this passage sets before us is that the One who does the shaking is God himself.</u> God shakes up the earth, shakes up the people.

I do not think there is any doubt that we are presently in one of those shaking times, and have been for several years. We have entered into one of those perilous times when all that we would normally have counted as strong and steady is being shaken and overthrown. I don't mean events such as we saw last week—the overthrow of the government of Chile. Such episodes have been almost continual in the record of human history. The toppling of thrones, the changing of empires, are really incidentals, not the essential developments. When I speak of the shaking of that which seems to be permanent I am talking about far more important matters.

WHAT ARE THE THINGS BEING SHAKEN TODAY?

What are the things being shaken today?

First, and probably most evident to us right now, is the great shaking occurring in people's confidence in human government. We have been involved in the Watergate investigations during these long summer months. Few of us have failed to see how that whole matter has served to inhibit and stymie and prevent the proper functioning of government. It has been like a huge, paralyzing hand laid upon governmental operations. And regardless of how you may view it, or what sympathy you may have for those involved, one thing is evident: Watergate has shaken the people's confidence in the operation of government. Men who were selected for high office and who people were confident would make moral decisions, have proven to be untrustworthy. Yet everyone knows that these wrongful decisions were ones that they themselves might have made, had they been put in the same offices. The weakness which has been manifested in Watergate is the kind which is difficult even to recognize when it is happening to you, and many of us might have gone right along with it.

2. DONALD TRUMP IS HAPPENING NOW IN 2022
THE BIG LIE
3. THE INABILITY OF OUR GOVERNMENT

The inability of our government, and of other governments in the world, to control the inflationary spiral, resulting in terribly high prices and the undermining of our economic foundations, has shaken people's confidence in government.

WE SEE OURSELVES IN THE GRIP OF ECONOMIC FORCES TOO VAST TO MANIPULATE OR CONTROL

We see ourselves in the grip of economic forces too vast to manipulate or to control. Even with the best of intentions and the widest of knowledge, men seem unable to reverse the trend of what is happening today. This represents a shaking of that which we thought to be solid and dependable.

THE WORLD OF SCIENCE AND TECHNOLOGY

You see the same effect in the world of science and technology. I remember a few decades ago when it was thought that all these new inventions coming so rapidly upon the scene would bring us tremendous progress in the solving of human ills and social problems. I can go back at least as far as the advent of television! Everyone thought it would be wonderful to have entertainment and newscasts right in our homes, merely to turn a knob and have the world in our living room. Now we know that television has brought a curse along with its blessing. Too much exposure tends to make us artificial, turns us into robots. We lose the capacity to develop our own creative skills of recreation and entertainment.

WE ARE EVEN MORE FRIGHTEN BY SOME OF THE OTHER THINGS SCIENCE HAS BROUGHT US SUCH AS ARTIFICIAL INTELLIGENCE and The MetaVerse.

SUCH AS ROBOTS, SOCIAL MEDIA AND SATTLE-LIGHTS AND CHARL DAWIN

We are even more frightened by some of the other things science has brought us, knowing that our cities are glutted with traffic, our skies darkened with smog, and our waters poisoned. No one seems to be able to stop it or to reverse it. We realize now that science has not been the benefactor we thought it would be, but has brought with it ills so tremendous they appear to be Frankensteinian monsters, threatening our very existence. This has shaken people's confidence.

AS YOU ARE WELL AWARE

As you are well aware, a very definite shaking of our time is evidenced in the change in moral standards.

MORAL VALUES

What we once thought were irrevocable, steadfast standards, by which any decent people would live, are now being challenged, overthrown, and cast out. We see a tremendous shaking in the very foundations of the nation, as families are breaking up and the divorce rate is skyrocketing—not only in those marriages of a few years' standing, but increasingly in those which have endured more than twenty years. And we wonder what is happening to our family life as, more and more, the philosophy of the day is that marriage is not important at all. "Unmarriages" are springing up all over, in which people choose to live together without any legal ties. There is widespread acceptance of this kind of arrangement. And sexual explicitness has come into the media, graphically portraying now what never would have been allowed in public even a few years ago. We see the shaking of the foundations in this area.

THE RISE OF THE OCCULT

And perhaps more dramatic than any other development today is the rise of the occult, the return to witchcraft, black arts, and the open and acknowledged worship of demons and dark powers which influence and possess men. The rise of outright demonic possession is being found on every side. I wonder if we realize what dramatic changes have occurred in our nation.

244 YEARS OF AMERICAN HISTORY

that as of the 4th of July 2020, the United States is 244 years old. It's 244-years-old because the Declaration of Independence was ratified by the US Second Continental Congress on July 4, 1776.

Look back across the 244 hundred years of American history and you find that at no other time in the history of this nation has there ever been this kind of outbreak of demonic powers such as white nationalism, ions, imposter Chirality, Critical race theory, Money problems, Tithing etc.

There has been a guard or shield over this nation, and other nations of the West, which somehow has inhibited and prevented this kind of attack. We could always have traveled to India and Africa and other places and found this, but now it is here at home in America. And California is the worst area of all. Why is this? It is part of the shaking of our times—-this dramatic breakthrough of demonic forces which is frightening people and giving rise to many new cults and bizarre practices.

As we look ahead we tend to be shaken ourselves by these shakings of the earth and of heaven. But this passage is intended to comfort us, for it says that this shaking comes from the hand of God. <u>It is God who shakes the heavens and the earth, not the devil</u>. He is only the instrument of God to do this. God is doing the shaking, and he is doing it for a very great purpose described for us in this passage:

"Yet once more I will shake not only the earth but also the heaven." This phrase, "Yet once more," indicates the removal of what is shaken, as of what has been made, in order that what cannot be shaken may remain. (Hebrews12:26b-27)

THIS IS WHAT GOD IS WORKING TOWARD

This is what God is working toward. He allows the shaking to come in order that what cannot be shaken may again become visible to men. One of the great encouragements of this day is to see that this is exactly what is happening. As the writer goes on to say, "Therefore let us be grateful for receiving a kingdom that cannot be shaken," he underscores one of the things that cannot be shaken today: the sovereignty of God.

THE TRUTH IS EMERGING TODAY IN A NEW AND FRESH WAY

This truth is emerging today in a new and fresh way, more than at any time in my memory, as men are beginning again to see God's hand in history, God at work among men. You can see this fact emerging in all these areas I have just covered. For instance, in the nation, as a result of the shaking of the confidence in men who were elected to office, and the resulting distrust of the democratic process, there is gradually coming into this nation once again a consciousness that righteousness and truth are important, and an acknowledgment that no nation can really stand unless it is based upon a people who love justice and righteousness.

WE HAVE LOST THIS FOR SOME TIME

We have lost this for some time. A decade or so ago a great wave of "super-patriotism" swept across this country. People began to run up flags and put reproductions of the Declaration of Independence and the Constitution on their walls. An effort was made to convince people that these were the undergirding of the foundations of our nation, that we had to look to these human documents to support this nation and make it strong and steady once again. But you don't hear much of this anymore, because God has allowed the foundations to be shaken, and men are now beginning to see that no human document is the explanation of a nation's strength. It is not the democratic processes or the Constitution or the Declaration of Independence that will hold us steady in the day of sweeping tumult. Rather, it is the righteousness and truth that people love which will do it, and the fact is that only men and women who are committed to these values can be trusted in the hour of pressure. Once again people are seeing this clearly.

The same is true in the realm of education and technological training. The revolt of youth just two or three years ago shook this nation, but it helped us to see that in educational processes we cannot indulge in the bizarre and untried. And although we must return to what has proven itself, the emphasis must no longer be on material values but on personal values—love and harmony and peace. The gauges of success are no longer big cars and expensive homes and luxurious provisions and furnishings, but rather a family which relates lovingly to one another, does things together, and shares life. These values are coming back into our educational system partly as a result of the shaking of our times.

Even in the realm of morals this shaking has produced tremendously helpful developments. The shaking of the foundations of sexual morality is now beginning to produce an awareness of the true purpose of sex. Even churches, which have been so dead and dull in this area are now beginning to take a healthy view of sex and to teach their people what it was intended to be. I walked into a Christian bookstore not long ago and stood there looking at all the books that were available on the subject of sex, books which were wholesome and biblical and helpful—and detailed, not in unwholesome, but in right ways. I rejoiced, for it took me back to my own early Christian youth when I was given the only book available to Christian young people on how to handle sexual drives. It was called The Way of a Man with A Maid. I read it again the other day, and I threw it down in disgust! It is one of the most perverted treatments of sex I think I've ever read. It distorts the whole biblical picture, makes sex appear to be dirty. Yet that was the commonly accepted textbook on sex when I was a young man. No wonder God shook us up in this area, and made us take a good look at what we had been thinking and the way we had been acting.

Out of the shaking is coming a realization of the things which remain and which cannot be shaken because they are based upon the fiat of God, the decrees of the Creator. One of the things which cannot be shaken is the realization again of the true nature of the church. It is so encouraging to see that Christian people are finally beginning to realize that the important thing about a church is not the building program. Just a few decades ago churches were knocking each other over to see who could come up with the most expensive, luxurious building. They were bragging about the softness of their carpets and comfort of the pews, the lushness of the furnishings, and the newness of the electronic marvels available for amplifying voices. Now, fortunately, we hear very little about this, for there has come a return to the fact that the church is not a building but people. It is the TECHNOLOGY OF GOD. A church is not functioning properly simply because it pays its bills on time and is able to send money to support a missionary program. It functions only when its people share a real and genuine faith, visible in their neighborhoods, when homes are being healed, when humanity is being fed, when drugs are put down, when demonic deliverance is being done through CHRIST JESUS, where THE HOLY SPIRITS SPEAKS AND WE LISTEN and families are coming back together, when long-standing arguments and divisions between church members are being broken down and AGAPE love is being manifested.

I have recently been in the northwestern states which, as many of you know, are a citadel of conservatism in churches. It was so encouraging to see that in place after place congregations are forgetting about emphasizing their minor doctrinal differences with other churches, forgetting about labels and titles and "reverends," and all this kind of nonsense, and are returning again to the emphasis of the New Testament. Thank God for the shaking, because it produces an awareness of the things which remain.

And this is true in the whole realm of righteousness. As I look back at the church as I have observed it through several decades of life, and if I try to see it through the eyes of the watching world, I see that what most people have observed in the church is self-righteousness —judgment and condemnation for certain practices, sharp and harsh words toward things which people commonly do. One of the most helpful trends of today is that this is disappearing. Some Christian people are now beginning to realize what has always been true—sin does not consist merely of drunkenness and lechery and licentiousness and sexual misbehavior. Far worse are criticism and bitterness and resentment and jealousy and quarreling among believers. And we stand under the judgment of a holy God just as much for these sins as do those outside the church for the others. We have not a finger to point nor a stone to throw.

People are coming back again to an awareness that the only righteousness God will accept is that based upon his forgiveness. If there is any area of our life in which we have never been forgiven, it is there we are offending the Spirit of God. If there is an area about which we are saying, "Well, I've never done that kind of thing; I wouldn't do that!" it is through this right there we are grievously hurting the Spirit of Truth. Righteousness consists of that gift of forgiveness which comes when one has known himself to be a sinner before God. That is why our uptightness about hair styles and modes of dress and bare feet is disappearing. Some of us are beginning to realize that these externals are not important; it is what we are in our hearts before God which matters. So the sovereignty of God and the centrality of the cross remain unshaken. The fact emerges again and again that human life is never realized until it comes to the end of itself. This explains the Jesus Movement, and all the other encouraging signs of the return of the life of the Spirit in America and around the world. Some of us are once again understanding that there is no hope in man. That is what the cross says: "No hope in man." God is doing his work. GRACE (GRACE IS DOING IT'S WORK) that is God's Riches at Christ Expense.

That is what is emerging more and more in the shaking of our time—that there is no hope in man, and there is no power in self, that dedication and discipline are not enough to find answers to the problems we face today or ever, that merely knowing the principles of life by which to act is inadequate, that the proper actions cannot be carried out except by a reliance upon the power of God at work within us to motivate us and empower us to do it. We cannot merely take a list of things which ought to be done and determine to do them. More and more the message of the cross is coming through to us: "There is no power in self." We cannot grit our teeth and clench our fist and say, "I AM GOING TO DO IT!" and get it done. We are like Paul, as he cried out in Romans 7, "For I do not do what I want, but I do the very thing I hate," (Romans 7:15). "Wretched man that I am! Who will deliver me from this body of death?" (Romans 7:24). Once again the answer comes—we are delivered by the activity of God at work within us: "Thanks be to God through Jesus Christ our Lord!" (Romans 7:25a).

Then the cross says, "There is no fear in love," (1 John 4:18). The answer to fear is to understand the love of God for us, and his availability to us. That is why Paul can exult as he does in Romans 8: "If God be for us, who can be against us?" (Romans 8:31 KJV). I love that, don't you? And as the writer of Hebrews puts it,

Keep your life free from love of money, and be content with what you have; for he has said, "I will never fail you nor forsake you." Hence we can confidently say,

"The Lord is my helper,

I will not be afraid;

what can man do to me?" (Hebrews 13:5-6)

Jesus answers his frightened disciples again and again: "Be not troubled." "Let not your hearts be troubled." "Be not afraid." "Fear not, for I am with you."

This is the word which cannot be shaken today. What should our response be? The writer of Hebrews says two things: First, "Therefore let us be grateful"—grateful hearts, praise and thanksgiving to God that we have a place to stand when all around is being shaken.

Has your home been shaken this year? Mine has. And it is great to have a place to stand which cannot be shaken. What praise rises from my heart to God for the unshakable things which cannot be removed!

When everything else begins to rock and shake, when our foundations are trembling and there is upheaval on every side, how grateful we ought to be for things which cannot be shaken.

Then the second thing—not only grateful hearts, but responsive wills: "Let us offer to God acceptable worship." Here we are gathered together to worship God. What will be acceptable to him? Certainly not perfunctory, mechanical worship. He doesn't want us just sitting here waiting for the meeting to get over so we can go do something else. Jesus said, "They who worship God must worship him in spirit and in truth," (John 4:24). Worship is the whole man aimed at God, the whole man looking toward him in thanksgiving and praise and not occasionally, but continually. As Paul puts it in Romans 12, "... by the mercies of God ... present your bodies as a living sacrifice, holy and acceptable to God, which is your spiritual [acceptable] worship" (Romans 12:1b)—bodies available to him, ready to respond to needs around us and around the world with AGAPE LOVE, to respond to the plea for help in the Sunday School, and to your neighbor's need for encouragement, and to your children's cry for direction and love, ready to respond to your husband in his hour of despair, and to your wife when she is feeling neglected and worthless. That is what the acceptable AGAPE worship of God is all about. "Let us offer AGAPE LOVE to God acceptable worship, with reverence and awe; for our God is a consuming fire." He envelops life like a great flame, burning away—either destroying us or purifying us. AGAPE Love is a fire. The love of God, touching our lives, is either going to burn us up and destroy us, break us apart in the shaking of the foundations, or it will steady us, strengthen us, establish us, and purify us, burning up the dross in our lives.

This is the God with whom we have to do. So let us come to life with grateful hearts and responsive wills in the name of Christ Jesus, in this hour of the shaking of earth and of heaven.

Once again, our Father, we are grateful for what your word reveals to us about what is going on in our life, in our families and homes, and in our nation and world. Help us to respond as this word suggests—that we not refuse him who is speaking, for we cannot avoid the shaking which is occurring. Lord, let us take a firm stand upon those things which cannot be shaken the AGAPE love and government of our God, the greatness of his being and power, and his mercy toward us—and with grateful hearts give thanks, and make ourselves available to you this day. We ask in Christ Jesus' name, Amen.

THE FOUR HORSEMEN OF REVELATION 6

Introduction

My friend said as he was preparing for his evangelistic meetings in Zimbabwe, he was going through all the sermons that were provided to him by Global Evangelism, making sure the notes went with the slides, checking Bible versions, and so forth. When he came to the sermon on the remnant church, I noticed that the sermon was built around Revelation 6:1-8. It interpreted the horses as representing various stages of the Christian church, but it gave no support for its interpretation.

Not having time to conduct a full study of the issue, he looked in several books and Bible study pamphlets for support for this interpretation. Nothing. He called his brother, who knows a lot more about prophecy than he does, and asked him. He didn't know, and his books turned up nothing. I ended up preaching the sermon as it was with a disclaimer, but it bothered him to give an interpretation of the Bible without solid support—even if the interpretation is correct.

Background

Revelation 6:1-8 is part of a larger context. First, it is part of the seven seals. This means that the four horsemen cannot be taken completely independently of the seals. Second, it immediately follows the throne room scene of Revelation 4, 5. Chapter 5 begins by describing a scroll sealed with seven seals and the search for someone worthy to break the seals and the scroll. The second half of chapter five describes Jesus as worthy to break the seals and open the scroll.

When chapter 6 begins, the setting is the same as the previous chapter. Jesus is breaking the seals one by one, and John is describing what he sees in connection with each seal. It is plain that what he sees is symbolic. Most of the imagery in Revelation is symbolic and there is no indication that this passage is different. Furthermore, a literal interpretation does not make sense, especially when all seven seals are considered.

Bible prophecy frequently deals with sequences of events. This makes it quite possible to understand the seals as a sequence of events.

Revelation 4-5 describes the enthronement of the resurrected Christ on the heavenly throne and the inauguration into his royal office, the event that took place at Pentecost. Thus, the opening of the seven seals begins with the inauguration and enthronement of Christ.

THE SECOND COMING

Yet the opening of the sixth seal describes the Second Coming and the events that accompany it (6:15-17). This suggests that the scene of the opening of the seven seals covers the historical era from the ascension of Christ… to the Second Coming.[2]

This gives a historical sequence to work with.[3]

The Horsemen

Revelation 6:2 describes the first horse and rider: "I looked, and there was a white horse! Its rider had a bow; a crown was given to him, and he came out conquering and to conquer."[4] Both Stefano Vic and Maxwell identify this rider with Jesus. Given the sequence of time, it most likely concerns the first century church, although Jesus' victories will continue until the end of time, as Stefano Vic observes.[5]

The Second Seal

The situation is somewhat more muddled in the following verses. Verse 4 says that when Jesus opened the second seal, "out came another horse, bright red; its rider was permitted to take peace from the earth, so that people would slaughter one another; and he was given a great sword." That this horse produces great violence is obvious. If we understand the seals as a sequence, it is easy to relate this seal to the time of persecution after the first century, when Christianity was outlawed by Rome. Although he does not connect this seal to a specific time period, Stefano Vic notes that persecution is the result of following Christ.[6]

Maxwell apparently sees this seal as referring to persecution of any kind that Christians face throughout history.[7] While it is true that persecution can and does happen at any time, this does not seem to be the natural understanding.

Third Seal

The third seal is described in verses 5, 6:

When he opened the third seal, I heard the third living creature call out, "Come!" I looked, and there was a black horse! Its rider held a pair of scales in his hand, and I heard what seemed to be a voice in the midst of the four living creatures saying, "A quart of wheat for a day's pay, and three quarts of barley for a day's pay, but do not damage the olive oil and the wine!"

This passage describes scarcity. According to Stefano Vic, a pair of scales symbolized famine in the Old Testament; the idea was eating bread by weight—rationing it.[8] However, all is not lost; olive oil and wine are untouched.

Amos 8:11 refers to spiritual famine—a shortage of God's words. Indeed, this has happened. The Bible was outlawed and people were expected to rely on religious leaders to know God's will. But as the oil and wine were not harmed, the Holy Spirit worked through the shortage; all was not lost.[9]

Final Horse And Rider

The final horse and rider is described in Revelation 6:7, 8. John describes "a horse whose color was pale green like a corpse. And Death was the name of its rider, who was followed around by the Grave. They were given authority over one-fourth of the earth, to kill with the sword and famine and disease [Greek: death] and wild animals" (verse 8, NLT). The result of spiritual famine is death. This is exactly what happened to the pre-reformation church. Corruption was rampant and churchmen were more interested in secular matters than sacred.

Conclusion

This paper has examined the historical sequence of the first four seals. However, the seals carry a practical application—a secondary meaning. Stefano Vic notes that the first horse depicts the spread of the gospel; the remaining three show the consequences of rejecting the gospel. "All these scenes," he says, "are drawn from the Old Testament, and they contain the permanent truth of what happens when people reject the gospel and choose to live in sin."[10]

THE BLACK HORSEMEN OF REVELATION

7.7 billion

According to 2 sources

How many people are in the world? Get this: You are one of approximately 7.7 billion people living on Earth right now, according to the U.S. Census Bureau. While just 170 million people made up the world's population 2,000 years ago, the human race has exploded in the centuries since.

The Black Horse of Famine

The food-rich countries' potential to feed the entire planet makes it hard to imagine a famine extensive enough to thrust the earth into a global crisis. Yet the third seal of Revelation 6, employing the symbol of a black horse, describes just such a horrifying scene. How could this happen? What would be its consequences?

Is it conceivable famine could spread to impact the wealthy, food-rich countries of the world?

People are—and have long been—suffering from famine in many parts of the world. Famine has returned to Ethiopia where more than 7 million are in desperate need of emergency food supplies in order to avert starvation. Perhaps another 2 million require immediate help in Eritrea.

For Africa as a whole, the United Nations' Food and Agriculture Organization (FAO) declared in March that 23 of the continent's 53 countries—almost half—face dire food shortages.

More than two million people have died in the past decade in North Korea due to food shortages caused by a combination of flood, drought and bad government policy created by Kim Jong Il, the nation's dictatorial ruler, who currently threatens the use or sale of nuclear weapons. Periodically he has used his threats to gain aid, including food and oil, from the world community.

The scourge of famine has appeared cyclically throughout history. Often it is caused by drought, blight, floods and other natural means beyond human control. At other times the causes are all too human—war, social unrest and breakdown, and inefficient or outright malevolent government policy.

In today's global society, there should be no real obstacle to alleviating the effects of food shortages wherever they occur. Modern agricultural methods and generally stable weather patterns produce bumper crops in the developed world resulting in massive levels of food production, more than enough to feed the hungry of the world.

There is no reason to expect people to starve when this is coupled with the means to transport food to any location in the world. Yet famine and suffering from food shortages continue—and at times even grow.

It's easy to dismiss famine when it's on the other side of the planet or some far-off, isolated corner of the globe. Is it conceivable famine could spread to impact the wealthy, food-rich countries of the world?

The third horseman rides

We have covered the meaning of the first two horsemen of Revelation 6—religious deception and war. We come now to the third horseman's ride. What does it portend for the world?

Notice what it says in Revelation 6:5-6: "When He opened the third seal, I heard the third living creature say, 'Come and see.' So I looked, and behold, a black horse, and he who sat on it had a pair of scales in his hand. And I heard a voice in the midst of the four living creatures saying, 'A quart of wheat for a denarius, and three quarts of barley for a denarius; and do not harm the oil and the wine.'" What does this mean?

The Expositor's Bible Commentary explains regarding this passage: "This amount [of money] suggests food prices about twelve times higher than normal ... and implies inflation and famine conditions (Matthew 24:7). A quart of wheat would supply an average person one day's sustenance. Barley was used by the poor to mix with the wheat."

Food shortages cause inflation in food prices. And higher prices make the remaining food harder to afford.

SYMBOLS OF PLENTY

Oil and wine, though, are typically symbols of plenty. The reference here could indicate there will be pockets of abundance in the midst of famine. Christ's reference to famine "in various places" (Matthew 24:7) indicates the same possibility.

The cry to not "harm" the oil and wine could represent attempts to safeguard the pockets of abundance against plundering. However, The Living Bible interprets the phrase in Revelation to mean that there is practically no oil and wine left. That would also fit with the admonition that what is left not be harmed—lest there be none left at all.

In any case, the opening of the third seal indicates the onset of a period of severe famine unlike any in the past. While famines of varying severity have struck throughout history, it appears things will get much worse. Most of us have seen pictures of famine in our time, usually in parts of drought-stricken Africa. In 1984, a famine in Ethiopia developed through natural means, but was aggravated by the unstable government. Millions were at risk of starvation.

Thankfully, a massive humanitarian effort from around the world stopped the famine from killing as many as predicted. (Even then, corrupt government officials withheld some of the donated food as a weapon to starve their political opponents.)

This was testimony to the generosity of the many wealthy nations and the global means of transport that is available. However, if a nation's social fabric begins to unravel, larger problems can set in. The crises in Africa may be a foretaste of larger tribulations to come.

Prelude to an apocalypse?

Food insecurity and outright famine is already a reality faced by hundreds of millions of people throughout the world. According to the UN report of covid-19's impact on food security, before covid-19, already 820 million people worldwide were considered as being "food insecure," of which 135 million were in crisis and emergency status. There has been slow, steady progress in the international effort to reduce those numbers and lift people out of poverty. But the large, worldwide economic interruption caused by covid-19 threatens to undo recent progress made and plunge more people on the brink deeper into a crisis of nutrition. It is estimated an additional 130 million people could fall into acute food insecurity by the end of 2020. Those impacted the most primarily live in South and Southeast Asia, with the majority of the remainder in Sub-Saharan Africa.

Exacerbating the major economic impact that threatens to plunge ever more into poverty are overlapping threats from rainfall patterns in east Africa causing floods, landslides and even fostering conditions for the ongoing locust swarms that are devastating the region. Abundant rains brought an earlier planting season at the beginning of 2020—a good thing—but also bringing about flooding, mudslides, flash floods, and river overflows that have displaced many people, damaged infrastructure and destroyed some crops. Meanwhile the locust outbreak that began in 2019 continued into 2020, hitting Ethiopia, Kenya and Somalia particularly hard. From the UN report: "Swarms of Desert Locusts there are extremely large, highly mobile, and are damaging food crops and forage. The Desert Locust is the most destructive migratory pest in the world. In response to environmental stimuli, dense and highly mobile Desert Locust swarms can form. They are ravenous eaters who consume their own weight per day, targeting food crops and forage. Just a single square kilometer of swarm can contain up to 80 million adults, with the capacity to consume the same amount of food in one day as 35,000 people. When combined with the covid-19, flooding and the spread of these locusts, East African people find themselves combatting a "triple menace"."

Even in nations where food security isn't as large of a problem, breakdowns in the supply chain have resulted in destruction or waste of perfectly good food simply because it isn't able to be delivered. "Border restrictions and lockdowns are, for example, slowing harvests in some parts of the world, leaving millions of seasonal workers without livelihoods, while also constraining transport of food to markets. Meat processing plants and food markets are being forced to close in many locations due to serious covid-19 outbreaks among workers. Farmers have been burying perishable produce or dumping milk as a result of supply chain disruption and falling consumer demand. As a result, many people in urban centers now struggle to access fresh fruits and vegetables, dairy, meat and fish."

Devastating famines of the past

Famine is listed in Revelation 6 as following the previous horsemen of religious deception and war. While nature—drought, floods and insect infestations—is often the cause of famine, quite often war and misrule, as well as malignant political or religious ideology, are prime factors. A look at past famines gives us an idea of how devastating they can be.

JOSEPH STALIN

During the 20th century two humanly engineered famines brought devastating consequences. In 1932-34, the Soviet dictator Joseph Stalin sought to suppress Ukrainian nationalism by forcing a system of collectivized agriculture on the peasants. Food supplies were removed to the cities, crops failed and food supplies were barred from the region. This manmade famine resulted in the starvation of between 6 and 8 million people. It was a state-sponsored attempt at genocide.

CHINA

China's "Great Leap Forward" in 1958-60 resulted in mismanaged food production and the disruption of distribution chains. Fertile rice fields were plowed over and factories built on them. Farms were collectivized. Farmers who knew only the land were at a loss in factories. Coupled with bad weather, the result was the death of 20 million people by starvation during 1960 and 1961.

Famine in prophecy

Let's step back in history to the book of Leviticus for a look at God's warning to man through the example of Israel. Here we can see the consequences of false religion, war, famine and pestilence when Israel was unfaithful to God.

Leviticus 26 is a chapter of promises from God—the promise of blessings for obedience and of curses for disobedience. The first step toward blessings is faithfulness in the worship of the true God. "You shall not make idols for yourselves; neither a carved image nor a sacred pillar shall you rear for yourselves; nor shall you set up an engraved stone in your land, to bow down to it; for I am the LORD your God. You shall keep My Sabbaths and reverence My sanctuary: I am the LORD" (Leviticus 26:1-2).

For keeping His statutes and commandments, God promises in the next verses the necessities for plentiful food production: "rain in its season" so that "the land shall yield its produce, and the trees of the field shall yield their fruit ... you shall eat your bread to the full, and dwell in your land safely."

Continuing, He says: "I will give peace in the land, and you shall lie down, and none will make you afraid; I will rid the land of evil beasts, and the sword will not go through your land ... For I will look on you favorably and make you fruitful, multiply you and confirm My covenant with you" (Leviticus 26:3-9).

BY LIVING RIGHTEOUSLY AND AVOIDING FALSE RELIGIONS

By living righteously and avoiding false religion, Israel would be able to receive divine blessings of good weather, fertile soil and plentiful rainfall. Peace, material abundance, good health and the absence of disease would follow. In other words, the curses like those accompanying the horsemen of apocalyptic disaster would not go through their land as long as they sincerely obeyed God and worshipped Him in truth.

AFTER THE RETURN OF CHRIST

This promise will be applied to all nations after the return of Christ. In time, they also will receive these same promised benefits when they, too, learn to live the way God has revealed in His Word. But until then, we will continue to see cyclical occurrence of famine, from all sorts of causes, resulting in millions of people dying when they could have lived.

Terrifying Look Into The Future

In Deuteronomy 28 God details the horror of a people stricken with the curse of famine. It demands our attention so we may understand what lies ahead for the world when the <u>third horseman rides.</u>

For disobedience, God says He would bring a nation from afar to besiege and blockade the cities. All the food stores would be forcibly taken. The resulting starvation would cause the social structure to unravel at a frightening speed. The results are horrifying to contemplate.

"You shall eat the fruit of your own body, the flesh of your sons and your daughters … in the siege and desperate straits in which your enemy shall distress you. The sensitive and very refined man among you will be hostile toward his brother, toward the wife of his bosom, and toward the rest of his children whom he leaves behind, so that he will not give any of them the flesh of his children whom he will eat, because he has nothing left in the siege …" (Deuteronomy 28:53-55).

Famine Induces Cannibalism

Famine-induced cannibalism is the lowest depth of depravity to which a nation can sink. Yet scenes like this have occurred in history — and God says they will happen again. Reading this in the light of today's reported tragedies is profoundly sobering. But such deeply distressing events inevitably occur when men and women become entrenched in their disobedience to God's laws.

Hope In The Midst Of Horror

Jesus Christ wept over the fate that was about to fall on Jerusalem in the first century. He knew that terrible scenes would occur within the "city of peace." He wanted to gather the people into a loving and protective embrace and keep them from such tragedy.

But their sins and defiant attitude would not allow them to repent and escape what was coming. So the only course left for them was impending desolation and the cruel lessons of experience (see Matthew 23:37-39). The worst horrors described above in Deuteronomy 28 fell on them during the Roman siege of Jerusalem. Those horrors will only grow as mankind continues its self-destructive course of rejecting God.

Nothing is more basic to human survival than food and water. Yet the entire world is wholly dependent on elements totally beyond human control—namely sufficient rainfall, sunshine, temperate weather and fertility of the earth beneath our feet—to keep us alive.

The many recurring reports of droughts, floods, losses of fertile land and disturbed weather patterns should wake us out of our complacency. Ultimately, we are dependent on God for everything. When He decides to pull the plug on the systems that support human life on earth, it will be too late to realize how much we've taken these things for granted.

One horseman is yet to ride in this grim scenario. We will see in our next installment that he rides in tandem with this third horseman. We have not yet seen the full depths of the catastrophe that awaits the world as the seals of Revelation 6 are opened and the human tragedies described in them unfold.

In His Olivet prophecy, Jesus gave the first description of the events symbolized by these seals—and His prophecy is unerring. He foretold that there will be a time of great tribulation, greater than any previous world conflict, and unless that time is cut short, no human flesh will survive.

No treaty, no cease-fire, no human being, will be able to stop this end-of-the-age cataclysm. Events will drive the world into an out-of-control spin. But for the sake of a remnant called "the elect," His true followers, "those days will be shortened" (Matthew 24:21-22).

Coming Of Jesus Christ

Too often, people speak of this period as "the end of the world" or by some other similarly gloomy name. Terrible as that time will be, the world will not end and human life will not be extinguished. The Bible gives us hope that the light will dawn out of the chaos at the end of this age. It is when we keep our eyes firmly focused on this truth that we can have hope beyond the tensions of our present world.

www.ingramcontent.com/pod-product-compliance
Lightning Source LLC
LaVergne TN
LVHW021050100526
838202LV00082B/5427